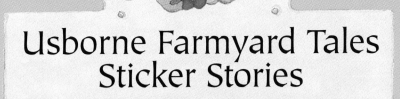
The Silly Sheepdog

Heather Amery

Illustrated by Stephen Cartwright

Language consultant: Betty Root
Series editor: Jenny Tyler

How to use this book

This book tells a story about the Boot family. They live on Apple Tree Farm.
Some words in the story have been replaced by pictures.
Find the stickers that match these pictures and stick them over the top.
Each sticker has the word with it to help you read the story.

Some of the big pictures have pieces missing.
Find the stickers with the missing pieces to finish the pictures.

A yellow duck is hidden in every picture. When you have found
the duck you can put a  sticker on the page.

This is Apple Tree Farm.

Mrs. Boot, the farmer, has two

called Poppy and Sam. She also has a

 called Rusty.

Ted works on the farm.

He has just bought a sheepdog to help him with

the  . The sheepdog is called

Patch. He is in the  .

"Come on Patch," says Sam.

"We'll show you all the animals on our farm."

 goes with Poppy and Sam. "Let's

see the  first," says Poppy.

They go to the hen run.

Patch jumps into the run and chases the

 . They are frightened and fly up onto

their house. "Stop it, Patch," shouts  .

"Let's go and see the cows," says Sam.

runs into the field and barks at the

. But they just stand and

stare at him. "You silly dog," says Poppy.

6

Then they go and look at the pigs.

Patch jumps into the pig pen and chases all the

 into their little house. Sam runs

to open the  .

Sam shouts at Patch.

"Come here . You silly thing.

You are meant to be a sheepdog.

will have to send you back if you can't be good."

Ted

I found the duck!

Poppy

I found the duck!

sheep

Patch

children

I found the duck!

Sam

boy

I found the duck!

sheep

boy

Rusty

Ted

I found the duck!

I found the duck!

grass

I found the duck!

tail

hens

truck

Patch

I found the duck!

hens

dog

I found the duck!

pigs

I found the duck!

sheep

hedge

Ted

Patch

I found the duck!

Poppy

I found the duck!

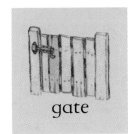

gate

I found the duck!

I found the duck!

boy

I found the duck!

field

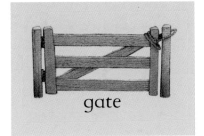

gate

I found the duck!

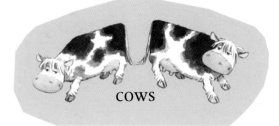

cows

They go to the sheep field.

"One of the 🐑🐑 is missing," says

Sam. "Yes, that naughty Woolly has run off

again," says  .

Patch runs away across the field.

Ted, , Poppy and run

after him. "Where's Patch going?" asks Sam.

"I don't know," says Ted.

Patch dives into the hedge.

He barks and wags his  . "What has he

found in the ?" asks Poppy.

They all look in the hedge.

11

Patch has found a boy.

The  pats Patch. "I wondered who bought

you when my Dad sold his farm," he says.

The boy has found a  .

"That's Woolly," says Sam.

"I found her on the side of the road, eating some

 ," says the  . "I was

bringing her back."

13

The boy whistles to Patch.

Patch chases Woolly through the 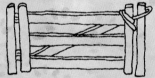 .

She runs into the  . Soon she is

back with all the other sheep.

Ted is surprised.

"Patch doesn't do anything I tell him," says

 . "You have to whistle to him," says the

 . He whistles again.

Patch runs back to them.

"You must teach us how to whistle to Patch," says

Ted. "He isn't silly after all," says  .